Written |
Sreelekha Kundu
Stacey A. Pawlak, PhD
Hanna E. Stevens, MD, PhD

Illustrated by:
Natalia Welzenbach- Marcu

I would like to thank Dr. Stevens and Dr. Pawlak for their support and guidance throughout the creation of this project, the illustrator for bringing my words to life, and my parents for their unending support.

- *Sreelekha*

Hi Mom, I'm here. Though it feels like I've been with you for years. Your soft voice and swift strides kept me safe, as I hid away in my comfy space.

Months have passed, I now lay in your arms. Far from harm,
surrounded by the familiar soft voice and warmth.
I'm so happy Mom. I'm so happy that I want to jump up and
down, skip across town. But I may need to wait,
until I have grown.

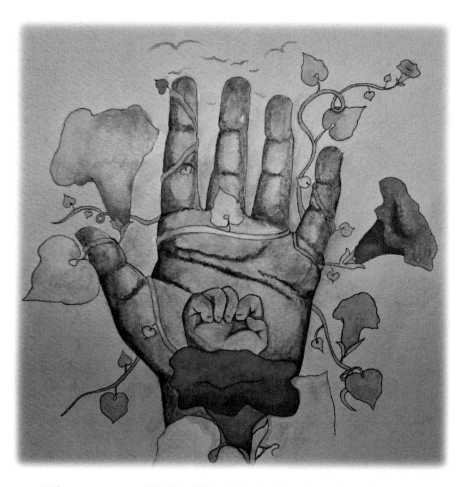

The years will fly like birds in the sky, but the memories we ferment will stick like a handprint in cement.

Tears and smiles. Anger and excitement. Feet to miles.
Support and judgment.
Sometimes rain, sometimes sunshine;
through it all, you will always be mine.

Yes, you are my mother.
There can never be any other.

However, never forget that you are a person
who feels fear and emotion.

There will be peace there will be commotion;
your mind will not always be as calm as the ocean.

There will be waves and we must be brave.
Your arms will tire, and you may even lose desire.
But through it all, we're in this together.

My ears are small and voice non-existent.
Do you feel sadness? Do not resist it.
Feelings are feelings, we must embrace it.

When I cry, you are nearby.
When you cry, take a step back,
even if you feel under attack.

Who is there for both you and I, go to them and tell them why. Tell them why rain streams from your eyes.

Tell them why fear clouds your mind.
Tell them why you feel so different;
remember that your feelings are
always significant.

The sun will shine, even after thunder.
When others give you help, I no longer wonder.

Life is new, for me and you.
A new beginning, with a whole new meaning.

Isn't it strange? A year ago you didn't know,
that it would be me who would change your world so.

How do you feel mom? Are you excited?
Do you feel joy with all other emotions uninvited?

Your mind and body are strongly linked.
You and I are forever synced.

Mind and body, body and mind.
The two are woven together, just like you and I.

A distressed mind may not be kind
to the resilient shrine that gave me life.

Up above the sky so high, like a diamond in the sky.
You sing to me, with your soothing voice.
I stare at you, so mesmerized.

My Mom, so strong and staid.
It is your strength that helps you look for aid.

You hum sweet tunes to calm me down,
and hold me tight, before I'm grown.
Years go by and I'll be by your side.
Together we will experience life, what a ride.

Behind the clouds there is a beautiful sun.
At the end, you and I will always be one.

My love for you will never run.
Forever and always, I love you Mom.

Welcoming a new baby is usually an exciting and joyous time, though this incredible life transition may bring unexpected feelings and emotions, too. While many parents experience mild mood changes during or after the birth of a child, up to 1 in 5 birthing persons experience more significant symptoms of depression or anxiety.

We encourage new parents to listen to what their minds and bodies are telling them and seek help, if needed.

Postpartum Support International (https://www.postpartum.net/; 800-944-4773) can connect you to online or local support options, but please call the National Suicide Prevention Hotline (1-800-273-TALK (8255)) if you are in crisis.

Made in the USA
Middletown, DE
26 June 2022

67805160R00018